LIBRARY
WITHDRAWN

KU-621-038

CONTENTS

1. The Kidnapping   1

2. Destination Unknown   6

3. Survival   16

4. The Wild Boy   26

5. The Flames   38

6. The Lake   48

7. Escape to Danger   61

8. Mine   70

9. Trapped   80

10. The Hard Way Out   88

11. Then   102

CHAPTER 1

The Kidnapping

With a violent crack, the front door jumped on its hinges. Then came two more blows and the door's wooden panels started to splinter.

Carlos watched it happen from the living room, his horror keeping him rooted to the spot. Someone was breaking into the apartment.

What the ...? Carlos thought.

His first instinct was to run to his bedroom window and climb out. But this wasn't his ground-floor apartment in the heart of Manaus. Here he was ten storeys up in a tower block on the outskirts of the city. There was only the shantytown and the rainforest below.

Mum's work took her deep into the Amazon and just now she was doing even longer hours, with all the wildfires burning. So Mum's boss had let her rent this dump of a place for a month so she could get back to Carlos after her shift more easily.

The door shuddered again from another blow.

I've got to call the police, thought Carlos. He jerked into life and started hunting about for his mobile. He ran to his room. Frantically, he searched the mess on the floor, on the bed, trying to find his phone. *Come on, come on ...*

Carlos felt a spike of anger that Mum wasn't here. He had hardly seen her over the last three days. He'd been stuck alone in the hot apartment, miles away from all his friends and bored out of his mind while stink and smoke blew in from this trashy neighbourhood. This was all Mum's fault. Mum and her dumb, stupid job.

"Don't go out by yourself," she'd told Carlos, "and you don't open that door for anyone but me! You hear me?"

All Carlos could hear now was the door giving way. It wouldn't stay standing much longer.

Feeling sick, Carlos ran to the built-in wardrobe in Mum's room and hid inside. The only outfit with any bulk or cover was Mum's spare uniform. Khaki top, stab vest, trousers, backpack and cap – this was the clothing of Captain Monica Feliz of the Special Forces Group of IBAMA, Brazil's environment agency.

Carlos shut his eyes. *While you're out protecting the Amazon, Mum, who's protecting me?* he thought.

The pounding at the door stopped. Sweating and shaking, Carlos felt his heart pound as a key slid into the lock. He heard the mechanism turn and the door swung open, squealing like a dying beast.

Why break the door down if you had the key all along? thought Carlos. For a short stupid second he thought it might be Mum. And yet he knew the heavy steps on the wooden floor weren't hers. Carlos was so scared he couldn't open his eyes, couldn't stop shaking.

I should've hidden near the front door so I could've dodged outside, he thought. Instead Carlos was shivering in the hot dark of the wardrobe, his eyes tightly shut, listening to the intruder thump around the apartment.

What had they come here for?

It had to be something to do with Mum's work. Carlos knew that what Mum did was dangerous – she had the scars to prove it and enemies that could fill a prison. One of them must have come here to—

"FOUND YOU!" the intruder yelled as the wardrobe door was yanked open.

Carlos opened his eyes to find a man in a black ski mask standing over him.

"You're coming with me," the man said.

Feeling desperate and terrified, Carlos tried to push past the man, but a big hand closed on the back of his neck. He felt thick cotton wool pushed into his face and smelt the sharp tang of chemicals.

Carlos closed his eyes.

They didn't open again for a long time.

CHAPTER 2

Destination Unknown

The sky was dark when Carlos woke. Not with night but with ... clouds?

No. It was smoke – a blanket of ash smothering the world.

Carlos stared up blankly, trying to make sense of where he was. He was lying on bouncing leather and his limbs prickled with pins and needles. His mouth was as dry as sand. The ground was lurching under him: Carlos was in a jeep, rumbling over rugged land.

With a jolt, Carlos remembered the man in the apartment. He tried to push himself up but found his hands were tied with rope. Carlos thrashed about, trying to right himself.

"Hey!" said the driver. "Cool it back there." The driver had short black hair and a thick moustache. He filled the driving seat, as solid as a sack of rubble.

"You're the man who took me," Carlos said, his voice croaky.

"Gee, don't tell my mum," the man said with a snort. "Pleased to meet you, Carlos Feliz. My name's Gedra."

Carlos ignored the greeting and licked his sticky lips. "Where am I?" he asked.

"Disney World," Gedra said. "Where'd you think?"

I'm in the jungle, Carlos realised. *The smoke must be from the forest fires.* He felt his stomach churn with panic. *How long have I been asleep? How far from Manaus am I?*

Gedra reached back to Carlos, holding out a half-empty bottle of water. "Drink this."

It was more of an order than an offer. Carlos took the bottle and drank the warm water, then splashed some on his face to wake himself up. "Why did you take me? What ... what are you going to do?"

"Don't pee your pants, kid," Gedra said. "We won't hurt you." The jeep hit a huge pothole in the track but rumbled on. "But your mum – Captain Monica Feliz – she just needs to stay out of stuff that doesn't concern her."

"What stuff?" Carlos demanded.

"You know what she does." Gedra smiled into the rear-view mirror. "You're going to make your mum realise that she needs to stop."

Like you could ever stop my mum, Carlos thought. Each day she left the flat saying,

"Sorry to leave you, kid, but I gotta go save the world." It was a joke they shared.

Gedra had made it sound like what Mum did was something bad. Most of the time, Carlos would've agreed. He hated his mum being away for so long, risking her life every day. She spent more time being Captain Monica Feliz than being there for Carlos.

And so she'd always tried to dress up her job like it was something out of a superhero comic book. She was the head of a special task force that policed the rainforest and had told Carlos about the "supervillains" she faced: the "Land-Grabbers".

These Land-Grabbers were illegally cutting their way deep into Amazonas, the part of Brazil where the world's largest areas of unbroken rainforest were found. They were farmers, loggers, miners. The statistics were crazy – an area of forest the size of a soccer pitch was lost every minute. So Mum and her team had the power to arrest these Land-Grabbers and destroy their camps and equipment.

They had to, before it was too late for Amazonas.

Carlos had had the reasons why drummed into his head for as long as he could remember. The Amazon rainforest was the so-called "lungs of the Earth". For centuries it had been sucking up tons of the carbon dioxide that humans pumped into the atmosphere. But as more of the rainforest was lost, the job it did wasn't just slowing down. It was going into reverse.

As they were destroyed, the rainforests were starting to breathe out the carbon dioxide they had held on to for so long. This meant climate change was boosted and the planet warmed faster. The problem grew worse with every tree that was felled, with every patch of forest that caught fire ...

For millions of people this destruction was a disaster to be fought and protested over. For Carlos it was simply something that took his mum away. Something that left him defrosting yet another meal for one in the microwave while he waited for Mum to get back. Some superhero she made! Carlos turned off the news whenever the trouble in the Amazon made the headlines, yelling, "Boring! Don't care!"

Now it seemed that Mum had messed with Land-Grabbers once too often and they were going to use Carlos to make her pay.

Carlos pushed his feet into the back of Gedra's seat. "How long was I asleep?" he said.

"Not long enough," Gedra growled.

"Where are you taking me?" Carlos asked.

"Shut your damn mouth."

Carlos stared out of the window, hoping to spot some sign or landmark.   But it was hopeless – there were only tall trees all around, their leaves strong and emerald green against the dark haze of smoke overhead. The Amazon rainforest was massive – if it were a country it would be one of the largest in the world. There had to be tens of thousands of fires raging across its vast green land. Some of those fires had been set on purpose to clear the land. Some had been started by accident. All of the fires were burning uncontrollably.

If I've been flown here, Carlos thought, *or taken by boat, I could be anywhere.*

The sky was growing darker with smoke as the jeep turned onto another track. Carlos spotted buildings behind a fence on the other side of the track. A farm maybe? If only he could get out and ask for help!

"I need to pee," Carlos said.

"Well, hold it," said Gedra, eyeing the smoke outside. "It's not so far now."

"Not so far to where?" Carlos asked.

"To your new home, Carlos. You're gonna love it. There's—"

Gedra broke off at the sound of a crash to the right of the jeep. Carlos stared as a stampede of cattle smashed apart a timber fence. Maybe thirty or forty of the panicked animals ran through the gap. One cow crashed into the side of the moving jeep. Gedra swore and swerved away from the stampede. Terrified, Carlos braced himself as the jeep skidded off the track. It tipped into a ditch with a nasty crunch of metal. The engine cut out, ticking noisily.

Gedra slammed his hands on the wheel. "That sounded like the axle," he said. The cattle were already rumbling on ahead, vanishing in clouds of red dust. Gedra's own door was jammed against the side of the ditch, so the big man had to struggle out of the passenger door. "I have to see how bad this is."

Carlos lay at an awkward angle in the tipped-up jeep, coughing as smoke and dust blew inside until the door swung back shut. Gedra crossed to the front of the jeep to look at the damage. Carlos looked out of the rear window, praying he'd see farmhands racing after the runaway cattle. People who might help him.

Instead Carlos saw fire – wild flames roaring to each other from the treetops on each side of the track. The fire swept closer at an alarming speed.

The jeep was going to be engulfed.

CHAPTER 3

Survival

The trees at the sides of the track exploded into flame. Horrified, Carlos yelled out to Gedra. But the big man must've already seen the fire, as he was bolting away down the narrow track after the cattle, holding a walkie-talkie to his ear. Thick black smoke gusted after Gedra as if giving chase.

Carlos was alone, trapped inside the jeep with his hands tied together. Smoke was already filling the car as he scrambled into the driver's seat. The ropes burned at his wrists as

Carlos managed to wind up the window just as the first angry orange flame licked at the glass. Then he closed the air vents, hoping that might keep out the smoke. Finally Carlos grabbed Gedra's discarded ski mask from the passenger seat. With some difficulty he splashed the remaining water over it and put it on the wrong way round to protect his eyes and cover his mouth from the hot, thickening air.

Carlos wriggled down into the footwell and curled up like a dog, trying to calm his breaths. He felt something sharp digging into the top of his leg but with the mask on he couldn't tell what. He heard the crack of glass. The metal car frame grew hot against his back as the jeep began to rock from side to side in the crackling flames. Thick fumes of burning rubber filled the air. Carlos choked on the filthy air, close to tears, wondering, *What if the fuel tank catches light and explodes?*

Every minute felt like an hour. But finally Carlos risked pulling off the ski mask. The jeep's windows were cracked and black with soot but the fire was weaker now – the bulk of it had swept away down the track.

If Gedra escaped, he could be back for me any minute, thought Carlos.

He pushed at the passenger door but it was stuck fast. Lying on his back, Carlos kicked against it with all his strength. Finally it opened. He clambered out, burning his tied hands on the smoking metal of the jeep.

The landscape had been transformed into a wilderness of ash. Smoke hung in the air like a poisonous mist and Carlos pressed the mask to his face again. No wonder those animals had been running so hard.

The jeep was a wreck, its tyres burnt to black jelly, its body steaming in the smoke. Carlos knew he couldn't risk staying here or running down the track. Gedra had told him they were nearly at his "new home", and when he'd run off he was using a walkie-talkie. People might already be out searching for Carlos.

I need to find cover, he decided. *I need to find out where I am and I need to get a message to Mum, or IBAMA, or something ...*

But what if the fires had driven everyone away? Where could he go?

Carlos saw the faint shadow of trees still standing through the ashy haze. He climbed over the cinders of the fence into the scorched earth beyond, heading for the trees.

*

Carlos thought he knew what to expect from the rainforest. Manaus was surrounded by it, and Mum had taken him to different spots over the years. But the wildness there had been tamed for tourists. After a day's tramping over worn trails, it was back to cool hotels, restaurants and free wi-fi.

Now, Carlos had spent hours struggling against the real rainforest and knew it to be a thousand times harder. It was an alien, hostile world without roads or paths, barely even a trail. Carlos longed for the city, with its clear streets and freeways, soaring buildings and tarmacked spaces. In the rainforest there was only a great shapeless tangle of nature. Branches and vines hung down on all sides. Butterflies flapped lazily by. Tiny jewelled hummingbirds darted past so fast they were gone before Carlos could turn his head. Every few metres something scuttled away into the undergrowth. At first he'd jumped with fright at every movement. Now he was worn down.

The sound of life was everywhere: chittering, rustling, hooting. But apart from

the odd parrot or monkey high up in the canopy, there was nothing to be seen. Carlos found it unsettling, like sensing a predator but not being able to see it.

And more than once he felt sure someone was watching him.

Already soaked with sweat, Carlos tried to press on faster through the trees and thickets and wildly overgrown scrub. At first he'd felt that the whole jungle wanted to destroy him but he'd realised it was worse than that. The jungle simply did not care. Carlos thought of how hard he'd worked since escaping and looked at the scars of his progress – the scrapes, bites and bruises. Yet on a map of the rainforest his progress would be shown as the tiniest dash of ink. How long could he go on like this with his hands tied? He might struggle on for days, growing weaker and weaker – just as much a prisoner as he had been in the jeep.

Again Carlos had the sense that he was being watched.

As he brushed against a tree he felt something hard press against the top of his leg. *I felt the same thing when I was curled up in the jeep*, Carlos realised. He reached into his pocket and found inside ...

A superhero figurine of T'Challa, king of Wakanda – better known as the Black Panther.

Carlos stared at the figurine, half wishing it could come to life and help him! Not that *this* Panther would be much use – its left leg had snapped off over the course of his ordeal. He felt a sharp pang of sorrow. He'd totally forgotten he'd been holding the Black Panther when Gedra had forced his way into the apartment. Carlos had stuffed it in his pocket, thinking it was Mum who was bursting in. If she'd caught him playing around with one of her precious superhero figurines, she'd have gone mad.

The figurines came with a magazine Mum got in the mail every fortnight but rarely found time to open. She would stockpile the magazines and now and then invite Carlos to help her carefully open the small cardboard box to reveal the superhero inside.

"They're not toys, Carlos, they're collectables," Mum always said. "You don't open one without me, OK?"

"Sorry, Mum," Carlos breathed aloud now. He pushed the broken figurine back in his pocket and felt like crying. He'd opened three of the magazines in the apartment just to spite Mum for being gone so long. What must she be thinking now? Had she called the police? Would anyone be looking for him? Mum always went on about how IBAMA's budget had been slashed – she was expected to police an area half as big as Britain with just a handful of officers. Even if they *were* out looking for him, how would he ever be found?

Carlos heard a stick crack behind him. He turned to find a hunched, misshapen figure stepping towards him.

CHAPTER 4

The Wild Boy

Carlos felt the hairs prickle on the back of his neck as he stared at the figure facing him. *I really was being watched*, he thought.

It was a boy: hunched over, dressed in a filthy checked shirt and frayed shorts. His face was scarily distorted and framed with a matted mass of hair. The boy's mouth was in a twisted sneer and his nose seemed to collapse in on itself. His right eye was barely more than a dark crack in his dirty face but the left eye was clear and fixed on Carlos.

"Mine," said the boy, his voice a deep grunt.

Carlos stayed very still. The word had been said in English, not Portuguese. Carlos didn't respond.

"Mine!" The boy waved an arm at the jungle, then at Carlos. "Mine."

Oh, god. He's crazy, thought Carlos. Carlos swallowed and said, "Speak Portuguese?"

The boy just stared.

Carlos tried again in clumsy English. "My name is Carlos."

"*Mine*," the boy repeated, then hurled himself at Carlos.

Carlos couldn't get away in time. He fell to the ground, struggling as the boy's twisted face pushed up against his own. Filthy fingers closed on Carlos's wrists and forced them over his head. Carlos yelled as ants burst from the ground and started crawling all over him. He closed his eyes, kicking to be free, but the wild boy had hold of his jeans, pinching and pulling at his pockets …

Suddenly the boy jumped away and retreated, his loping walk more like a monkey's than a man's. Carlos scrambled up from the mulch, brushing frantically at the green insects swarming over his arms and neck. The boy was covered in ants too but he ignored their swarming and crouched by a tree. He turned something over in his fingers, gazing at it like a jeweller might study a fine gem.

Carlos stared. *He's got Mum's Black Panther*, he realised.

"Mine." The boy gave Carlos a warning look and pointed to himself. "Davi."

"Davi?" Carlos said slowly in English. "Your name is Davi?"

The boy nodded, looking down at the broken figurine. "Davi."

Carlos tried to think clearly. Where the hell had this guy come from? He didn't seem all there, and his face ... What had happened to him? Carlos knew that there were indigenous tribes here in the rainforest, of course. The Land-Grabbers often set fires to try to drive them off their ancient plots so they could turn it into farmland in their absence. Maybe this kid was from one of those tribes? If Davi could lead Carlos to his people, perhaps there would be someone there who had a way to contact the outside world so Carlos could be rescued?

I need to make friends, thought Carlos. He still had the Panther's broken leg in his pocket. He swallowed hard, took a step towards Davi and offered him the broken limb. "Here," Carlos said.

Davi looked up at Carlos's hand with his one good eye. Then he grabbed the leg in one sharp movement and studied it in silence.

"Have you been following me?" Carlos asked. English was one of his better subjects but it took him time to put the words together. "Have you ... seen men looking for me?"

"No." Davi shook his head. He was fully absorbed in putting the broken leg in place, then pulling it away again, then putting it back.

Good, thought Carlos. He tried again. "I am lost, Davi. Where is ... your family?"

Davi got up abruptly and walked away, looking down at the treasure in his hands.

"Wait!" Carlos yelled, starting after the boy.

As Davi walked, his feet seemed to find their own path through the dense forest. Carlos realised that this was the boy's world –

familiar, taken for granted. Yet Carlos felt under fire from the cacophony of sound, heat and colour all about him. There was the barking of the howler monkeys and the stirring of birds, high up and invisible in the canopy. The pure blue of giant butterflies as they drifted their way from unknown blooms. The rustle of wet leaves by his feet as a snake slid slowly nearby. The sheer volume of life around him was overwhelming.

Minutes passed slowly, the time tearing at his nerves. Hugging himself, Carlos realised he was horribly thirsty and longed for the bottle of water from the jeep. *Still*, he thought, *Davi's tribe must have plenty to drink. They'll help me.*

"How far?" Carlos called. "How far away is your village?"

Davi ignored him and stopped beside a thick tree. Its trunk was a gathering of bony folds that rose up from the ground. Davi pulled a small knife from his pocket. Carlos took a step back, anxious, but Davi only used the knife to prise a hole in the trunk from which drops of thick goo bubbled out.

What the hell? thought Carlos. Then Davi dipped the broken end of the Black Panther's leg in the sticky sap and pressed it to the

figurine's stump. The leg stayed put and Davi held the figure up, triumphant.

"Right. You fixed it," said Carlos. "Great." He held out his hands to show Davi that they were tied. "Can you use your knife to cut me free?"

Davi stared blankly at Carlos.

"Help." Carlos strained to pull his wrists apart. "Please!"

Now Davi walked towards him, holding out the knife in a threatening way. Carlos wanted to back off but held his ground. Davi frowned at the ropes, as if noticing them for the first time. He put the blade against the ropes and sawed quickly.

"Thank you," said Carlos as the ropes broke away. His wrists were red and raw but it felt so good to be untied. In English he said again, "Please, how far to your village?"

Davi had turned away and was back gazing at his work on the Black Panther as if he were Michelangelo admiring the Sistine Chapel. "No village," the wild boy said. He nodded round to the jungle that hemmed them in. "Mine."

"You mean ... there's no one with you? You are alone?" Carlos felt sick with disappointment. "Well, where is the nearest place people live? There must be somewhere?"

Davi looked away sharply and crossed to another tree. This one held clumps of broad leaves with pointed tips. Davi pulled down on a branch and water trickled out from inside the leaves like a weird jungle water fountain.

At the sight, Carlos ran over. "Thank god – I'm so thirsty!"

But Davi turned sharply and pushed him away. Carlos slipped and fell on the wet stinking floor.

Carlos stared up at him. "What the—?" he began.

"No noise," Davi said.

"Oh, *what?*" Carlos felt so weary as he got to his knees. He spoke aloud in Portuguese, more to himself than to Davi. "I don't know who you are or where you came from but come on. *Please.* I was kidnapped. I don't know where I am or how to get home and you ... Come on, you've taken my mum's figurine. I let you have the whole thing and now you won't even share a few drops of water?"

Davi was staring past Carlos, his head tilted as if listening to something only he could hear. Suddenly there was movement in the canopy of leaves overhead. Carlos looked up and caught dark, fast movement in the branches. When Carlos looked back, Davi had turned and was crashing away through the leaves and branches, quickly lost from sight.

Carlos stared after him. "Fine," he called angrily. "I'll find a way out of here without you. Freak!"

There was only silence in reply. A silence that was unnatural here in the rainforest. The bird calls and the croaks and the chirrups had all stopped.

"No noise," Carlos muttered, remembering Davi's words. Had the wild boy been talking about the sudden quiet? Carlos looked around, uneasy and exhausted. He knew that no one good would ever find him in the middle of this dense vegetation. An IBAMA search would have to be done by helicopter, so he had to find some clear ground, someplace where he could be seen.

But first things first: his throat was parched. Carlos got up and did as Davi had done, pulling on the branch. He stuck out the tip of his tongue gingerly and licked the waxy surface of the nearest leaf. The water tasted of ash but still Carlos lapped at it thirstily.

Ash?

Carlos frowned. The jungle was still silent, as if holding its breath. He looked up but couldn't see much past the towering treetops. Ash from the forest fires would have blown for miles and miles, falling like dirty snow across the jungle. But if the wind was blowing this way …

It could be blowing the flames this way too, Carlos realised.

He sniffed and caught the scent of earth and wetness.

And of smoke, drifting across the forest.

And Carlos heard, close behind him, the greedy crackle of fresh flames.

CHAPTER 5

The Flames

Davi burst through the bushes back into the smoky clearing. He gestured to Carlos with one arm as if to say, *Come on! This way!* and sprinted back the way he'd come.

Carlos ran after him, his heart thumping, already feeling the heat of the fire at his back. Davi was so swift it was hard even to keep him in sight, let alone catch him up.

A troop of capuchin monkeys came bounding past, hooting with terror. One of them used Carlos's arm for a springboard and he froze, surprised. But surprise turned to shock and fear as a wildcat sprang from the green shadows, a blur of black and yellow. It raced out of sight, running for its life.

The crackle of flames was building higher behind Carlos. Did Davi know a safe way out? Carlos chased after him, crashing between the leaves and branches, driven by some primitive instinct to fly from death as fast as he could. He brushed aside webs that stuck to his face and spiders that clung to his hair. Sweat stung his eyes as it poured over his forehead. Carlos fought his way past thickets of thorns that tore at his clothes and skin, and his breath came in ragged scrapes.

To his horror, he saw the crimson shadow of flames closing in from his left. He panted for breath, shielding his eyes as the fierce orange inferno drove out the colours of the rainforest – the vivid jungle green, the blue of the butterflies, the bright palette of the parrots, toucans and hummingbirds.

Carlos turned and ran on, his breath catching in sobs now, a stitch digging at his side. The jungle was becoming a furnace, walls of blistering heat closing in on him. The whole world was burning down and he fell to his hands and knees.

"Help!" he screamed.

The forest floor was alive with insects. A brown patterned snake whirled past the leaves at his ankles in frantic S-shapes. Carlos realised suddenly that the faster creatures were fleeing the fire – like the monkeys, cats and birds. The slower ones could try to hide, to burrow into the ground or take refuge in water and try to wait out the flames and smoke.

But to do nothing meant death. And right now, Carlos was just one more animal fighting for his life. He crawled forward, choking and gasping.

"*Here!*" Davi shouted, appearing through the smoke, beckoning to Carlos.

Carlos summoned the last stubborn dregs of his strength, got up and pushed on past the vines and brambles towards Davi ...

And, like a miracle, the trees suddenly vanished. Hard sunlight speared down past the billowing clouds of smoke as Carlos staggered out onto a wide blackened clearing. This part of the forest had already burned, and long ago, judging by the dry skeletons of trees and the mulch of ash and mud.

Carlos knew from Mum that a lot of wildfires were set deliberately by Land-Grabbers – to clear the land for logging, or farming or cattle ranching, or otherwise to cover evidence of their illegal activities. But the fires often got out of hand. The dead

clearing here stretched on and on like a long grey scar across the jungle. It was a no man's land that stood safe between the walls of flame simply because there was nothing left there to ignite.

Carlos stared dumbly into the raging fires. The Amazon was home to so many wonderful things: thousands of rare species, plants that could hold an entire ecosystem in their leaves, incredible animals and natural medicines that might save countless human lives. The rainforests brought diversity to the planet, so much colour and life.

And what have humans brought to the rainforests? thought Carlos. *Fire. That's all. We brought the way to burn it all down.*

Still shocked, still choking, Carlos turned and followed Davi down the open stretch of wilderness.

There was nowhere else he could go.

*

The dead hillside grew steeper the further they descended. For some time Carlos could hear only the trudge of his footsteps in ash and mud but then sounds of life crept back into his ears – from the jungle that survived around the great scar.

Carlos remembered his mum saying that fire travelled faster uphill, since the flames could jump and spread more easily within the rainforest's canopy. Perhaps this low-lying area would be safe from the flames for a while. Perhaps that was why Davi was heading straight for the jungle now.

"Do you know where we're going?" Carlos called. "Or are we just on a nature hike?"

Davi gave no response, just kept up his steady loping walk maybe ten metres ahead.

"People are looking for me," Carlos called. "I need to stay out of the jungle so they can see me. *See me*," he emphasised, pointing to the sky.

But Davi wasn't looking. Of course he wasn't. He was pushing through the thick leaves into the cover of the rainforest.

Then a thought struck Carlos. Out in the open, a rescue helicopter would likely take a while to find him ... but Gedra would spot Carlos in a second.

Shuddering, Carlos followed Davi into the thick vegetation. The sound of swarming life was now a welcome contrast to the unnatural silence of the clearing. Even so, while he wanted to love the wildlife, he couldn't stop thinking of the danger: of bushmaster snakes, spiders the size of his head ... and the mosquitoes that hummed around him, loaded with tropical diseases. They probably killed more people here than any other creature.

The track Davi took was clear and well worn. It was a relief not to have to fight the jungle as he moved. Carlos was sore and tired to his bones. His legs and arms were a mass of cuts, scrapes and bruises.

Eventually the narrow track opened up onto a small gloomy clearing. A small wooden hut stood rotting in one corner, half caved in. A pile of decaying blankets lay in the low branches of a tree – Davi's bed presumably. Bowls of water stood at the base of the tree, covered with pieces of muslin to keep insects out. Davi took one of the bowls and drained it thirstily. Then he picked up another one and held it out to Carlos.

"Drink," he said.

Carlos took the bowl greedily. He swallowed the warm water so fast he choked but it was still sweeter than anything he could remember. "Thank you," Carlos said.

"You're welcome." Davi said it without any emotion. He pointed to the floor. "Sit."

Carlos scuffed at the ground, unsure. Was it safe? The area here was covered with leaves but he tramped carefully across the space several times and nothing leaped out of the mulch.

"Bad boy," Davi snapped impatiently, and his misshapen face bunched up tightly. "Sit."

Carlos was about to react, when he realised that Davi couldn't have plucked these words out of the air. Someone else must have said them. Someone who had treated Davi like a dog – someone who didn't seem to be here any more.

Carlos looked at Davi, who was sat by his tree, staring again at the Black Panther figurine.

Just who are you? Carlos thought.

CHAPTER 6

The Lake

There was a lake close to Davi's camp. Carlos only found this out when he followed Davi later that afternoon to see where he was going.

In fact, Davi was going to bathe.

There was something pathetic about the way the hunched figure of Davi stripped to his smalls and folded his tattered clothes in such a neat pile. But when Davi dived into the lake he was like an expert, barely troubling the surface of the still, dark water. It gave Carlos the confidence to wade in and join him. He left his clothes on but it was still bliss to sink into the cool water and soothe his burns and cuts and aching muscles.

The day was ending and Carlos watched the sunset as he lay back in the water. The reflection in the lake was like a mirror of deep red, broken only where the tall palms that lined the bank cast long shadows far out on the water. Flamingos and parrots winged by, on their way to their nests for the night. Carlos felt something like peace.

At least until his stomach rumbled.

"Davi!" Carlos said, pointing to his stomach and asking in English, "You have food?"

Davi swam across to the far side of the lake and pulled himself up onto the grassy bank. He crossed to some bushes and, to Carlos's surprise, pulled out a pink-and-white striped plastic bag. "Food," Davi replied.

Carlos climbed out of the water and walked round the edge of the lake to see. Davi pulled a bundle of banana leaves from the bag and passed it to Carlos. Inside the leaves was thick sticky rice with plantain and a spicy guacamole. It was cold and tasted a bit funny but Carlos wasn't about to turn the meal down.

"Did you make this?" he said as he swallowed a large mouthful.

Davi shook his head. "Mine," he replied.

Carlos frowned. "Well, thanks for sharing. But did you make it?"

"Mine," Davi said again, and pointed to a row of large palm leaves.

"I don't get you— *ugh!*" Carlos yelped. He jumped and saw a thick black leech had attached itself to its leg. "Oh my god, that is gross."

Davi stooped over, pinched the thin end of the leech and slid a finger under it to detach that end from the skin. He repeated the process for the fat end and flicked the leech back into the water before it could reattach itself – as calmly and easily as Carlos would've scratched an itch.

"Thanks, man," Carlos said. He wondered what worse horrors lay beneath the surface of the silent lake. *I've got to get out of the jungle*, Carlos thought miserably. *But without Davi, what chance do I stand?*

Davi had sat back down, his attention fixed now on whatever else was inside the bag. The crimson colour had faded from the sky as the sun sank and darkness closed in. The moon had risen and cast eerie silver shadows over this alien world. Davi tugged from the dirty carrier bag what looked to be half a burrito. He peeled away some waxy paper and stuffed the food into his mouth.

Carlos frowned again. Davi might have found the plastic bag somewhere, but how could he make and wrap his own burritos? This food had been properly packed and prepared – it reminded Carlos of street food in Manaus.

"Where did you get all this?" Carlos asked.

"Mine," Davi muttered, yet again.

Well, that's just not true, is it? thought Carlos. But he didn't want to upset his new friend. He'd most likely be dead by now if not for Davi and didn't hold out much hope of surviving the night without someone who knew the ropes here.

Davi suddenly jumped up and stuffed the plastic bag up into some forked tree branches. He brushed against the huge palms behind him and they swayed. Even in the poor light, Carlos could see that these weren't living palms – the branches had been stacked there like a tall windbreak.

Or like a barrier.

Carlos started towards the palms but Davi stopped him. "No. Mine. Dangerous."

"They're just branches."

"Mine," Davi insisted. "Dangerous." He pointed in the direction of his camp. "Home. Back."

"Back," Carlos echoed wearily. He thought of his mum. "Yeah. God, I wish I *was* going home."

*

The boys returned to the camp. Davi tied his flimsy hammock between two trees in the clearing and lay there, turning over the Black Panther figurine in his hands.

"Where do I sleep?" Carlos asked, shivering in the cool night air.

"Sleep," Davi replied, and pointed to the ground.

Carlos closed his eyes. "Ask a stupid question and you'll get a stupid answer."

He lay down at the base of the tree. Davi was asleep in seconds, snoring softly in his hammock, his gentle whistle adding to the croak and chitter of the surrounding wildlife. A breeze carried across the clearing. Carlos wished for long sleeves and a pair of jeans. With so much skin exposed he was vulnerable to every scratch and bite the jungle could offer.

For Carlos sleep felt as far away as home. Time crawled like a sloth. He nodded off a couple of times – for how long he couldn't tell – but he kept waking with a jolt, swiping at his neck in case something had crawled there.

This is too miserable, Carlos thought. The old hut was broken down but it would surely offer some shelter. Why didn't Davi sleep in it?

Perhaps he didn't need to – Davi was at home here in the open, fast asleep, his face softened in the moonlight's silver haze.

Slowly, carefully Carlos got up. He pushed open the door to the hut silently and flinched at the sound of things scuttling. Carlos took a grim step inside and banged his head on a metal object hanging from the low roof. Something light fell from it with a rattle. He groped around on the floor and realised it was a box of matches.

Carlos wasted no time in trying to light one. There was a scratch, a spark, and the very first match took. In its flickering light he saw he'd knocked down an old hurricane lamp.

By the end of the fourth match Carlos had managed to light the lamp and a soft orange light fell on the shadowy corners. A man's cobwebbed clothes hung on hooks in the wall beside a small framed photo of a smiling woman. There were English books on a shelf: a big Bible and others about religion, judging by the covers.

Carlos realised that he was standing inside the remains of somebody's home.

The last book on the shelf was a journal of some kind, written in English. Carlos picked it up, intrigued. His tiredness faded as he became absorbed in trying to translate the journal as best he could.

It seemed the author was a doctor and ... what was the word? A missionary: someone whose church had sent him to bring Christianity to tribes in the Amazon. This missionary had built the hut as a place to help sick people with western medicine. He had found Davi, who'd been thrown out by his tribe and left to die in the forest – probably because of the way he looked. The missionary helped make Davi well, taught him English and manners, and took him on trips up and down the river to show the other forest dwellers how the power of the Lord could heal, how it could make bad into good.

But something must've happened to the missionary, because the journal suddenly ended. The last entry was over a year ago.

Carlos put the book back on the shelf, his heart heavy with sadness. *Poor Davi,* he thought. *Abandoned, saved – and then left alone all over again.* Still, at least the missionary had left some clothes behind ...

He was just struggling into a damp long-sleeved shirt when the hut door was kicked open and someone burst inside. Carlos jumped at the sudden movement and knocked against the lantern.

It was Davi who had entered. In the dim and shifting light, the wild boy looked almost demonic as he lurched into the wreck of a room. His rage and pain were clear on his scarred, distorted face.

"Sorry!" Carlos cried, caught red-handed. "Sorry I came in here without asking." He struggled to think of the right English words. "This is ... private place? This is your ..."

"World," Davi said, tears leaking from his good eye. "World burn down."

Carlos looked past Davi. Red flames were weaving past the silhouettes of the jungle trees.

The wildfires had caught up with them.

CHAPTER 7

Escape to Danger

"Oh, you're so kidding me," Carlos said, biting his lip. He'd been shut away in the hut, wrapped up in the journal – he knew he'd have stayed unaware of the fires until the whole hut had burned down. Now he looked at Davi. "Run," Carlos said in English. "We run now."

Davi just stood there, his shoulders slumped, defeated. "World burn down," he muttered.

"We have to get away!" Carlos took Davi by the wrist and dragged him outside, carrying on in Portuguese. "Run or we'll burn like everything else."

"Mine," Davi said.

"No," Carlos snapped. "You're wrong. This place is not yours. It belongs to everyone. The rainforests are the lungs of the Earth and they belong to everyone. But I don't want to die here."

Already Carlos could feel the powerful heat from the advancing wall of flames. He thought of the poor, desperate, terrified animals who'd be displaced or killed. "Davi, we can't stay. We must get to the lake so the flames won't get us. Can you lead us there?"

There was no answer. Davi was still holding the broken Black Panther.

"*He* wouldn't give up," Carlos said, and stabbed a finger at the Panther. "T'Challa would fight – you understand? He fights for good. He saves things."

He grabbed the missionary's clothes and dumped them in Davi's lap. "Take all this stuff! It doesn't have to burn."

He looked at Davi and struggled to compose the English. "We go to … the big water place, you know?" The flames were eating through the jungle darkness like a child through candy. "Come on," Carlos said. "We're gonna be cut off!"

Davi wouldn't even look at him.

"All right, how about this?" Carlos shouted. He snatched the Black Panther from Davi's grip, leaving the wild boy holding just the leg. "You fought me for this thing before. Catch me and we'll fight again!"

Carlos stumbled outside, holding the lamp in front of him, heading in the direction of the lake. He risked a glance backwards but he couldn't see Davi at all. Feeling sick, Carlos stumbled on. The smoke jagged at his lungs like needles and he prayed he was on the right path.

Carlos emerged from the forest. The dawn sky was edged with grey-gold, lighting the smoke with eerie grandeur as it rose to meet the clouds. Panting, Carlos saw the lake. But he remembered the way the flames had consumed the space around him back in the jeep. To be trapped out in the open as the thick smoke filled the air ...

Maybe there was an alternative?

Carlos stumbled round to the far side of the lake and swept away the tall palm fronds that Davi had placed there to protect the space.

With the palms gone, Carlos found he was looking across to a camp at the base of a hillside.

Carlos had to rub grit from his watering eyes to be sure he wasn't dreaming it. No, there it was – actual signs of civilisation! It was like one of the shantytown shacks on the edge of Manaus, only smaller. The camp huddled in front of the tall rainforest trees that hid the world beyond from view. At least until the fires spread down there too.

"So, *that's* where you got the food," Carlos said, speaking to an imaginary Davi as he looked at the carrier bag still sitting in the tree. "And you didn't want the people down there to see you and maybe come looking." He gazed back across the lake, hoping to see Davi following him. But there was only smoke and a flurry of shrieking birds as they escaped the treetops. He looked down at the broken Black Panther still gripped in his hand.

"I have to get down there," Carlos told the small figure. "Someone there might have a radio. And there might be firefighters. I can get help for Davi ... get back to Mum."

Carlos stuffed the figure into his pocket and made his way down towards the settlement, wondering what sort of a place it would be. Considering how deep it was into the rainforest, it was probably illegal.

Look for the vehicles, Carlos thought. Mum always said she could tell what stage of deforestation an area had reached just by looking at the trucks. The first stage meant plenty of earth-moving equipment and trucks that hauled timber to clear the forest. Stage two would involve big cattle trucks, when the farms and ranches were set up. Finally, the soy tankers would move in – once the cattle had reduced the pasture to patchy scrub, the land was given over to growing soybeans. Then the cattle farmers would move on to burn down more forest for pasture and the cycle would begin again – trashing the rainforest to make a profit.

From what he could see, Carlos could not reach a conclusion. The only vehicles seemed to be 4x4s and motorbikes. Motorbikes were often the easiest way to travel large distances over ranch land but there were no big tankers for feed, nor any livestock containers. Perhaps the wildfires had been started by farmers burning their land to give nutrients back to the soil, and the flames had gotten out of control?

As Carlos made his way down the wooded slope he could see a whole gang of workers. They were digging a wide ditch at the base of the hillside – a kind of dry moat designed to stop the spread of the fire. They had to be trying to protect the lush forest around the camp.

Carlos moved faster as the slope began to level out. But there was a mass of thick, thorny scrubland in his way and he had to circle it, taking him further from the camp. More smoke came drifting towards him. Carlos felt cold sweat on his neck and back as he saw more crimson flames swarming at the brush that lined another narrow track. More people were tackling the fire, some using eight-foot poles with car-mats on the end to try to beat out the flames in the under-brush. Others squirted water through hoses from tanks on their backs. But against the sheer crackling magnitude of the flaming inferno, they were like children using fly swats and water pistols.

All the crazy statistics Carlos had heard on the news about how much rainforest went up in smoke each minute made hard and horrible sense. And these people who were fighting it with whatever they could weren't wearing the yellow uniform of the federal firefighters. They were risking their lives for free. They were heroes.

Carlos finally reached the foot of the hill and collapsed onto the dusty track. Blinded by the thick smoke blowing towards him, he got up and staggered away from the fire, heading towards the gang he'd seen digging the ditches.

"Help!" Carlos shouted, his muscles cramping. He could barely crawl now. "Please, I need help ..."

A figure of a man appeared from out of the swirling storm of smoke and ash and stood over him. "Don't worry, son," the man said. "We'll help you." A scarf was wrapped around the man's face and a cap protected his head. He put his hand to the scarf and tugged it down.

Carlos stared up into the smiling face of Gedra, the man who'd kidnapped him.

CHAPTER 8

Mine

Carlos woke painfully with no idea where he was. It took several seconds for the memories to drag themselves into his mind.

He quickly wished that they had not.

Carlos was lying on a small sofa as sunshine filtered through tatty orange curtains. A house? No, it was an old caravan. He heard a throbbing, chugging sound from outside rumbling like endless thunder.

Carlos was surprised and ashamed when he realised he'd needed no drugging this time to fall asleep. Utterly exhausted, he'd fallen into dark, fitful dreams from the moment he'd been dumped in the back seat of a Land Rover that stank of cigar smoke.

Now he was here in the caravan, alone. Carlos looked out of the window.

It was as if he had been picked up and dropped on the surface of the moon.

Carlos could see no jungle, no vegetation of any kind. There were only mountains of stones and lakes of muddy water beneath the threatening orange-grey sky. Large wooden pontoons hovered on the lakes like vast mosquitoes. They were fitted with long pipes stuck down into the water to suck it up like lifeblood. More pipes sprayed thick brown sludge onto rickety wooden slides that were perched on piles of rock.

A half-empty bottle of water stood on the counter and Carlos drank thirstily. His brain was beginning to make sense of what he was seeing. He remembered pictures on Mum's work laptop. And suddenly he realised what Davi had been trying to say in front of the palm fronds that kept his hideaway from view.

"Mine. Dangerous."

The poor guy hadn't been totally crazy and insisting that everything around him was "mine". Davi had been saying that down below was a *mine*. Same word, different meaning.

"Dangerous" was right for sure, thought Carlos. He knew that he was looking out on an illegal gold mine – one of maybe thousands in the Amazon. He'd heard his mum say that a lot of the drug gangs had moved into gold because it was more profitable than drugs. The soil and the rivers held plenty of gold dust but you had to destroy everything to get at it. Mum called it mining by brute force – cheap, uncaring and violent. And, of course, Mum was the superhero trying to shut the things down.

But how could anything stop this? Carlos stared at the endless movement of the mine with horrified fascination. He didn't understand what each different part did but he could see the end result.

Total destruction. Miles of lush jungle turned into pits of gravel for the traces of gold they contained.

Heart thumping, Carlos noticed men gathering at the bottom of rickety wooden slides. The slides were overflowing with muddy water. Some men pulled mats from inside the slides and stuck them into wheelbarrows. Others placed fresh mats into the slides.

Carlos crossed from one window to another at the rear of the caravan so he could keep watching the men push the wheelbarrows along the barren rocky track. They stopped beside what looked like an old paddling pool. The mats were carefully shaken and beaten over the paddling pool. Something was being collected …

The answer came to him in his mum's voice: "Gold dust."

He remembered her talking about it in their living room one day, looking down at a ring on her finger. "People give gifts of gold to show how much they care for the ones they love," she'd said. "But they have no way to know where that gold came from – whether forests were killed to produce it ... and bad people made rich."

The memories faded as Carlos noticed a man in a straw hat standing inside an old oil drum. Sludgy water from the paddling pool was poured inside and the man started to splash around in it like it was the world's smallest hot tub. What the hell was he doing?

Carlos gave up surveying the strange scene and considered his closer surroundings. The caravan door was locked, of course, and so were the windows.

But the small skylight in the ceiling was open a crack.

There was no freestanding furniture in the caravan that Carlos could stand on, so he scrambled onto the narrow kitchen counter. From there he could lean across to nudge the skylight open further with his fingertips.

He took a deep breath, gripped hold of the small ledge of the skylight and then jumped from the counter. He fought to pull himself up, thinking of the pull-up bar that was bolted into his bedroom doorway at home. He could manage ten reps on that, sometimes. But the skylight's ledge cut into his fingers – it was hard to get a proper grip.

Carlos put his head to the skylight and it tilted open as he struggled to pull himself clear. The gap was narrow and his shoulders barely fitted but in the end he managed to scramble out onto the caravan roof. He rolled over and lay face down, catching his breath, praying no one would find him out here.

The noise of an oncoming engine took his attention. Carlos raised his head and saw that a jeep was winding its way along the bare track towards the caravan. He felt fear like a fire in his chest.

But then the jeep stopped fifty metres away and the passenger door swung open – and everything changed.

Carlos couldn't believe he recognised the man who was climbing out.

It's Sergeant Edson, he thought. Edson was Mum's friend and fellow officer in IBAMA's Special Forces Group. The two soldiers had worked together for years, and partied together too. Edson had even bought Carlos his first bike, after Dad had moved away.

I've been found, he thought. Carlos felt actual tears of relief. It would be all right. Edson was here and IBAMA would shut down the mine. The nightmare was over.

He was about to yell out to Edson when he saw who else was getting out of the 4x4. And suddenly, despite the lazy heat of the day, Carlos felt stone cold.

It was Gedra.

Edson had been driven here by Carlos's kidnapper.

CHAPTER 9

Trapped

Edson and Gedra were talking and as they drew closer to the caravan Carlos could overhear them.

"... you botched this job from the start, Gedra," Edson said. "The police know a key was used to open the door to the kid's apartment."

"It was taking too long to kick it down," Gedra protested. "It was broad daylight. People were starting to notice me."

"So you let yourself in," Edson went on. "Which means Feliz suspects that Carlos was taken by someone she knows. If she ever finds out it's me ..."

"That craphole flat is rented," Gedra argued. "Anyone could have a key. It still sends her the message that if she knows what's good for her, she'll stop her tours of duty round here. We can get her stupid kid any time we choose."

"You think Carlos is the one that's stupid?" Edson spat on the floor. "It was you who managed to lose him on the way to the safe house."

"That safe house is ashes by now, boss!" Gedra said. "The fires are too strong; we can't stop them—"

"No excuses," Edson said, pointing a finger right in Gedra's face. "I'm being paid to keep these gold mines off IBAMA's radar. If the rainforest around here burns to the ground, there'll be no cover … And if just one federal plane flies overhead to drop water on the fires, they'll see all of this." Edson waved his hands at the mine around them. "Not *everyone* can be bribed to look the other way …"

Carlos shrank slowly back out of sight. There it was then: the reason for his kidnapping. His mum couldn't be made to turn a blind eye, so she had to be scared into staying away by having her son taken. Gedra must have gotten the key for their apartment from Edson. "*We can get her stupid kid any time we choose …*" The thought was terrifying. Even if he could get back, Carlos knew then that he'd never be safe.

"Go in and check if Carlos is awake," Edson said in a lowered voice. "If he is, blindfold him. He can't know I'm involved. If it really *is* Carlos you've picked up."

"I'm telling you, I got the right kid," Gedra insisted.

"No more mistakes, Gedra. Another boy was spotted hanging around the mine this morning … I need to be certain that's really Carlos in there."

Another boy? Carlos felt his heart thump so hard it could have hit the caravan roof. *Maybe Davi got out of the jungle? He knows the mine; he's stolen food from round here …*

Carlos pushed himself over to the far side of the caravan and dropped down as quickly and quietly as he could. He heard Gedra fumbling with the key to the caravan door. He knew he only had seconds before his vanishing act was discovered and the alarm was raised.

So Carlos ran like hell – off the track and down along the rocky slopes. He tried to go silently but his every step sent stones skittering away at a horrible volume. He heard shouting – Edson's voice. Carlos sped up, trying not to fall. Tears were biting at the back of his eyes. How was he ever going to get home now?

And how much would it take to turn kidnapping into murder?

Out of breath, Carlos reached the bottom of the stone slope. The mine workers had not yet reacted to his escape – the *chug-chug* of the generators that powered the suction pipes must have covered the noise of Edson's yelling. But it only took one bored mine worker to look up from their task and spot him ...

Carlos practically hugged the stone pile, trying to keep out of sight as he scuttled round its outside edge. He froze as he saw Gedra up on the track above him.

The man hadn't noticed Carlos yet, but held a gun in his hand.

Carlos spotted a hole in the rocky bank next to him. It looked as if the soil between two of the larger rocks had been scraped out by an animal. As quickly and quietly as he could Carlos wriggled and wormed his way into it and

pulled a rock behind him to hide the opening.
He crouched there in the mud, barely daring to
breathe. He heard more footsteps on the stony
track and the clatter of loose rock, holding
his breath as pebbles piled up in front of the
entrance to his hiding place. It felt like he was
being buried alive.

A heavy boot stopped in front of his
hide-out.

Then the man moved away again.

No one else trod across the great stone slopes near him. Carlos stayed hidden there for hours. A siren went off at one point – not the police but like an air-raid siren, calling all the miners to leave their posts and search for the missing boy. The generators powered down and Carlos could hear men patrolling past. He wondered how long he could stay hidden. His stomach was growling, his limbs felt stiff with cramp. And yet the fear of discovery kept Carlos frozen, the thought of Gedra's gun and what it might mean for him scaring him into stillness.

Finally the generators cranked up their chugging again as the normal work of the mine resumed. The search for Carlos must have spread further out, into the jungle beyond.

What if Edson is setting lookouts and roadblocks? Carlos worried, tense within his hide-out. *Even if I get away, I'll still be trapped.*

On foot, I don't stand a chance. I'll never get away ...

Then Carlos heard the slow squeak of a wheelbarrow and the sound of unhurried footsteps approach. *It's all right*, he told himself. *Doesn't sound like they're looking for you—*

But they were. Carlos flinched as the rock he'd used to hide the entrance to the hole was pulled away and he was dragged out into the daylight. Blinded by the brightness, Carlos opened his mouth to scream.

CHAPTER 10

The Hard Way Out

As Carlos tried to shout, a hand clamped down over his lips, smothering his words.

Carlos blinked as he saw Davi staring down at him.

"I don't believe it!" Carlos said, grinning. "I was afraid the fire got you. But you've risked your life to get *me*!"

Davi ignored him, dug quickly into Carlos's pocket and took back the broken Black Panther figurine. As Davi held it again, the tension drained from his face and his mouth twisted into a smile.

OK, so you came back for T'Challa, thought Carlos, and he almost laughed out loud. He closed his eyes for a moment, feeling sick from the adrenalin surging through him. When he opened them, he saw the man in the straw hat behind Davi – the one who'd been working with the oil drum. Up close Carlos could see swellings in the man's neck and an angry red rash over his face. The man was standing beside a large wooden wheelbarrow half filled with mats. Alarmed, Carlos grabbed Davi's arm and pointed.

But Davi shook his head, intent on trying to stick T'Challa's leg back to his body again. The man in the straw hat lifted up some of the mats, making a space for Carlos to hide inside.

"Why would you help me?" Carlos said simply.

"I've helped Davi for months," the man said. "Put food his way." A striped carrier bag, like the one Davi had hidden up by the lake, was tied to the belt of the man's shorts. "Clothes, too, poor son of a ..." He nodded to his barrow, unsmiling. "Get in."

"In," said Davi. He put the Black Panther figurine back in his shorts pocket and curled up tight in the small space. Carlos lay down close beside him. The stink of Davi's sweat and the earthy odour of the mats that the man piled on top of them turned Carlos's stomach.

"These mats pick up the gold dust from the muddy water, don't they?" said Carlos.

"That's how it works," the man said quietly. Carlos could just hear him over the rasp of Davi's breath and the squeal of the wheel as the barrow started moving. "The dust goes in the oil drum with the water. I add some mercury and splash around to mix it together. When you mix mercury with gold dust, it binds it together. Makes something solid."

"Isn't mercury poisonous?" Carlos asked.

"Very." There was no emotion in the man's voice but he had to pause to catch his breath as he struggled with the extra weight in his wheelbarrow. "But when it's done, we get a nugget of gold and the waste mercury is dumped in the river. The fish eat it. People eat the fish ..." The man paused again. "I know Davi's people. He's the way he is cos his mum got sick with mercury poisoning. Plenty children in that tribe were born sick. Plenty died."

Carlos couldn't believe what he was hearing. Of course Davi couldn't understand a word.

"The mercury did this to him?" Carlos asked.

"It's killing me too," the man said calmly. "I'm exposed to hundreds of times the safe level."

"Then why do it?" hissed Carlos.

"Cos I earn more in a week here than I'd get in four months anywhere else. When I'm dead, my kids will get enough money from me to be able to move away. Far from here."

Davi shifted under the mats, muttering. Carlos shushed him. He wondered where they were going, how much longer it would take.

The man spoke up again. "They said your mama works for the military."

"For IBAMA," Carlos said hoarsely. "She would close this place down."

"Bosses won't let that happen. Gold's worth three times more to them than drugs." The man paused again, wheezing for breath. "You know that man of God who helped Davi? He found out about the mine and the mercury in the water. Tried to warn the people. Bosses had him killed."

Carlos felt a prickle down his spine and closed his eyes.

"Enough people have died already," the man went on. "Why should they kill you and Davi too? Life's too short already. Just get the hell out of here, OK?"

The barrow tipped up suddenly. Carlos and Davi tumbled out alongside the mats, landing in the dust and blinking in the light. The man with the straw hat had brought them to a brown and stagnant pool in a crater cut from land that once teemed with life and colour. Dozens of mats hung from makeshift washing lines made from ropes tied between poles.

"Stick to cover where you can," the man said. "They still hunt for you." He pulled the carrier bag from his belt and tossed it to Davi. Carlos could smell the spicy food inside.

Without another word or backward glance, the man limped off to pull mats from the line under the gloomy sky as if nothing had happened.

Carlos did as the man said, Davi following just behind him. They stayed low, using the drying mats as cover while they could. Then they sprinted over to the first scrubland at the edge of the mine – finally some proper cover. But as he pressed forward, Carlos realised: "I don't know where I'm going." He stopped, turned to his companion, spoke again in English. "You go first?"

Davi lowered his head like a mournful dog. "Go where?" he said.

It hit Carlos then: Davi couldn't lead him anywhere now. The forests he'd known his whole life ... they weren't there any longer.

His whole world has burned down, thought Carlos. *He's like a lost kid. Davi only came after me cos he wanted that stupid Black Panther. Now it's the only thing he's got.*

It was as if Davi was listening in to his thoughts. "Mine," Davi said. "Gone."

"I know," said Carlos. "I am sorry. Maybe you can come with me?"

Davi looked up and stared at Carlos, no emotion on his face. "With you?"

"To my home. Manaus. It's a city," Carlos explained. "My mum will help you. I know she will."

Davi shook his head. "Home ... mine."
He turned in a slow circle, his arms raised.
"Here. Mine."

"But it's not yours any more, is it?" Carlos said angrily. "It's been taken from you. If you come with me—"

"Fight," said Davi suddenly.

Carlos frowned. "I don't want to fight you."

"Fight. Mine."

"You can't fight these people, Davi." Carlos thought of Edson's betrayal and closed his eyes. "You just can't."

Davi pulled out his broken Black Panther and held it like a club. "Fight!" He pointed between Carlos and the figurine. "You said. Fight."

"Only to get you to move!" Carlos said. Feeling sick and tired, he turned and stomped away through the jungle.

Davi shouted after him and sounded close to tears. "You said fight!"

"The Panther isn't real," Carlos yelled back. "He is from comic books. He can't fight for you. Now, we have to go—"

A jangling metal clatter erupted around them, the sound ear splitting, echoing over the thin green strip of forest. Carlos jumped, terrified. He'd blundered into a tripwire, which in turn had pulled down a net full of old pans and tin cans.

An intruder alarm, Carlos realised. *One that works going out of the mine as well as coming in.*

How many of Edson's friends were already on their way to investigate?

"You have to run, Davi!" Carlos shouted, charging away into the undergrowth. Was it his imagination or could he already hear the roar of a motorbike heading their way. "Davi, I said, *run!*"

Davi ignored Carlos and simply stared round, fearful, clutching the figurine close to his chest.

"Come on!" Carlos bellowed.

The next second a man on a dirt bike burst through the scrub, his head down. He steered over the uneven ground, speeding towards Carlos.

Davi jumped at the man with a shout of anger, smashing him off the bike.

The bike went swerving out of control. Carlos hurled himself aside as it smashed into a thicket. The tangle of plants held the bike there, its engine still running.

Carlos staggered back up and tried to lift the bike clear of the brush. It was a chance to get away – their best and maybe only chance. He called to Davi above the whine of the engine, "Get over here!"

Davi stared down at the still body of the man he'd brought to the ground and screamed out his anger: "Fight!"

Then he turned and marched into the forest, in the direction the dirt bike had come from.

"Come back, Davi! There's too many of them," Carlos shouted helplessly.

He waited. The throb of the dirt bike's engine was like the hum of Carlos's heart.

Davi didn't return.

Carlos took a deep breath. The air was starting to taste like smoke. The fires must be closing in, just like Edson's men. There would most likely be others searching the roads around here, looking for him.

All I've done since I came here is run away, Carlos realised.

He thought of Davi. Thought of the broken Black Panther.

The throb of the mine generators still carried through the thickening smoke. Carlos got on the bike and rode it shakily through the patchy forest.

And he didn't stop.

CHAPTER 11

Then

For the rest of his life Carlos would remember the three days that followed. Days he spent pushing himself to extremes.

Mostly, when he talked of it, he told the story as a great adventure: driving the bike cross-country, not daring to take proper tracks or roads until he was miles and miles from the mine.

Changing course each time he smelled smoke blowing across the trembling trees or saw the lick of crimson fire past the canopy.

Dumping the bike when its fuel had gone and trekking ahead on foot. Eating fruit and nuts from the forest, praying they weren't poisonous. Sleeping in trees. Waking to find a huge spider on his chest – and on one occasion an actual black panther prowling the mulch around the tree beneath him.

If only Davi had been there to see that.

Carlos talked of being chased on foot for miles by more wildfires blazing through the forest and his relief and disbelief when finally he chanced upon federal firefighters trying to contain the flames. The firefighters radioed for transport to take Carlos to the civil police station in Autazes, sixty miles away. They contacted his mum, and an IBAMA helicopter was soon on its way to collect him.

His telling of the story would usually end with his reunion with his mum outside the police station. They were both a mess of tears and snot as they held each other close after so long, having been certain that they would never meet again.

Carlos worked with his mum to pinpoint the location of the illegal gold mine. But it turned out that the forest fires and the military had already solved that problem. The jungle around the mine's borders had burned to nothing, leaving it exposed. The military had noted it during their fly-bys to drop water on the endless blazes – but by the time they went in to seize and confiscate, everything had gone. The gang had cut their losses and moved out.

For a long time the rest of the story was something Carlos rarely shared with anyone.

Carlos didn't talk of how much he'd missed Davi's company in those lonely, frightened days and nights on the run. How he'd lie awake wondering what had become of the boy he'd hardly understood but who had still saved his life.

Carlos didn't mention the real reason why Captain Monica Feliz left IBAMA's Special Forces Group. Edson had been careful not to leave any evidence of his involvement but Carlos's mum knew she couldn't trust her junior officer – that he was crooked and took bribes. She knew that she couldn't guarantee her son's safety if she went on with her work.

"Don't run away like I did, Mum," Carlos had begged her.

"I choose you over the planet," his mum had said.

He'd kept on: "Don't run out on the forests like I ran out on Davi, Mum. Fight!"

"There are lots of ways to fight," she'd said.

His mum had resigned from IBAMA the next day.

They'd moved away to São Paulo, a smaller city. Carlos's mum became a spokesperson for an environmental charity that promoted sustainable land use in the rainforest, helping farmers to make better, kinder choices that would keep trees standing. She rented a little apartment where her superhero figurines finally made it out of their packaging and onto a shelf.

Carlos kept a place reserved on the shelf for the missing T'Challa, the Black Panther. From time to time he would check on eBay, trying to buy one for Mum's birthday or Christmas. Each time he was outbid.

One day, nearly a year after his ordeal, Carlos came back from school to find his mum sitting with tears in her eyes and the biggest smile on her face. An old friend of hers from IBAMA had forwarded a package to her with a note attached:

You said you were missing the Black Panther in your kooky Marvel collection, right? Well, it's the weirdest thing. Our officers responded to reports of indigenous forest in Amazonas being chopped down for timber. They found an illegal sawmill burned to the ground, totally destroyed. On one of the tree stumps, they found this thing. Who knows how or why it got there, or what it's been through, but maybe you could use it as a free placeholder till you get a better one ...?

"It's come back to us," Mum said.

*

Most nights after Mum had gone to sleep, Carlos slipped out of his room and picked up that battered, broken Black Panther figurine. He traced his fingernail across the break in the

leg, glued messily back in place with rubber
sap. He studied the word carved in bad English
into T'Challa's back:

FITE

Maybe Davi had written it to inspire others. Maybe Carlos had inspired *him*.

*

Carlos is older now. His mum still campaigns to fight the wildfires devastating the Amazon, while he's planning to join IBAMA's Special Forces Group just as she did.

To fight to protect and restore the rainforest.

To keep the lungs of the Earth working.

Carlos knows that it takes everyone – whoever and wherever they are, however old. *Everyone* has to stand up and say: "MINE. The rainforests are mine. They stand for me, they stand for life. And I will stand and fight for them."

"This is war," Carlos says. "And war is like a fire blazing bright. It is terrible but it can help you to see. It opens your eyes to what needs to be done."

For your own sake, for mine, for all of us.

Do it.

Why I wanted to tell this story

World Burn Down is a work of fiction, but the problem of the deforestation of the Amazon is very real. There is an environmental agency in Brazil called IBAMA which works to protect the Amazon, but the government has reduced its power, and its work is getting harder and harder.

The Amazon rainforest is still home to indigenous tribes like Davi's, but they are constantly threatened by Land-Grabbers, who value gold, tin and magnesium in the ground over human lives. The miners they employ bring illnesses and pollute the rivers, driving the indigenous people from their homes.

Of course, our instinct is to run when we're faced with something huge and scary. When I showed friends *World Burn Down*, one of them said, "All Carlos really does is run from one danger into the next."

And this is exactly why I wrote *World Burn Down*: I wanted to show that Carlos is trapped inside the situation, just as we all are when it comes to climate change. He runs for as long as he can, but in the end Carlos knows that he must fight. Davi reaches the same conclusion. Carlos's mum seems to be running too, but she finds another way to fight by campaigning and spreading awareness.

A lot of us would rather turn away from the sad and terrible disasters in the world than face them, but we can only keep running for so long. Some problems are too big to go away. And if we let the rainforest be destroyed, the problems are going to get worse.

Luckily there are many ways for us to fight for the planet. We can try to buy second-hand furniture instead of new stuff so there is less demand for wood. Hold on to your phone instead of upgrading. Check supermarket labels so you can avoid buying food that contains palm oil and beef products that are not certified by the Rainforest Alliance.

Charities like WWF, Rainforest Foundation and Greenpeace are helping rainforests by working with the people who live and work there. They help them to farm the land more responsibly as well as grow new trees to replace those that have been lost. Perhaps you could think of ways to raise money for charities like these?

Environmental activist Greta Thunberg said, "When your house is on fire, you don't wait a few more years to start putting it out." This fire is a scary image. But by coming together with others and standing up to the problem we can make a difference. Each positive action is a win.

So, never feel helpless. Spread the word. The fire of climate change must be put out before the world burns down, and we're the only ones who can do it.

Our books are tested
for children and young people by
children and young people.

Thanks to everyone who consulted on
a manuscript for their time and effort in
helping us to make our books better
for our readers.